THIS BOOK BELONGS TO:

Splosh!

Mick Inkpen

Hodder
Children's
Books

A division of Hodder Headline Limited

'Splash!'
went the rain
on Kipper's umbrella.

'Splosh!' went the puddle as Kipper jumped into it.

'FLASH!' went
the lightning.
'BOOM!' went
the thunder.

'Drip, drip, drip,'
went the water off
the hedgehog's nose.

'Hop, squelch!
Hop, squelch!
Hop, squelch!'
went the three
little rabbits.

'A A A TISHOO!'
went the hedgehog.
And then he did it
again!
'ATISHOO!'

'Slop slap!
Slop slap!'
went the water
under the umbrella.

And at last,
   without a slap,
or a slop, or a hop,
   or a squelch, or a drip,
or a boom, or a flash
   or a splosh,
      or a splash. . .

. . .out came the sun!